The story of a little mouse trapped in a book

S0-BSC-393

STORY AND PICTURES
BY MONIQUE FELIX

© 1980 BY EDITIONS TOURNESOL-CARABOSSE S.A.
025, SAINT-SULPICE SWITZERLAND
A STAR & ELEPHANT BOOK
FROM THE GREEN TIGER PRESS
LA JOLLA, CALIFORNIA 92038
ISBN 0-914676-52-0